Trains

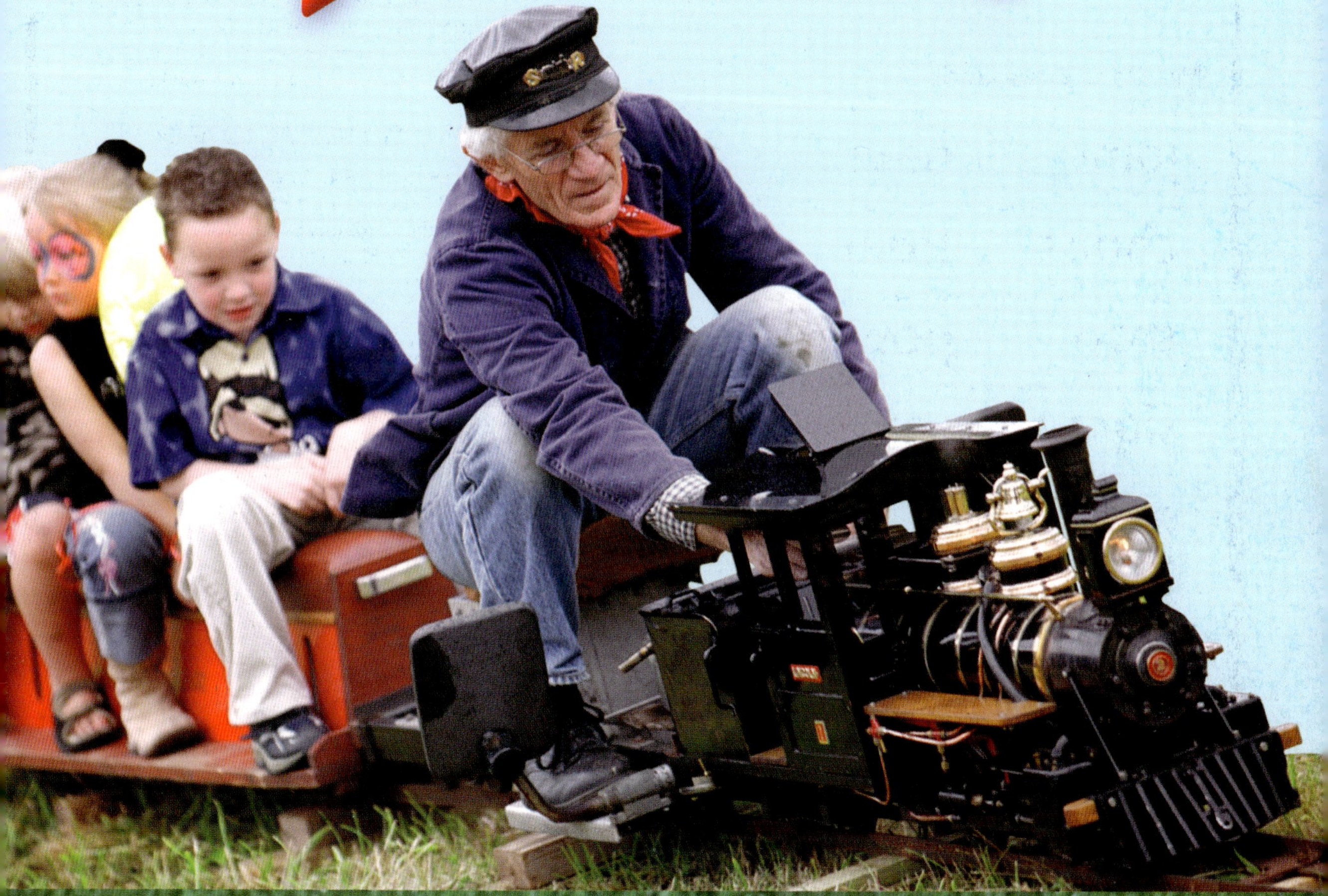

Written by Emma Lynch

RIGBY

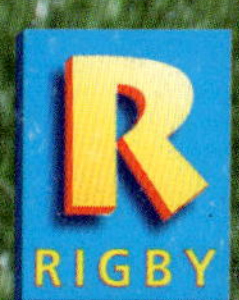

This is a train.
Trains run on tracks.

Tracks are metal rails.

Signals and lights tell the train to stop or go.

This light tells the train to stop.

Some trains have a cab and coaches.

Metal links join up the coaches.

We can go in this train.
The coaches have chairs for us.
They have racks for bags.

Some trains have beds for us to sleep in.

We cannot go in some trains.
Some trains are goods trains.

Goods trains, like this train, do not have chairs.

This train has trucks.
The trucks cart coal.

Long ago, trains got power from coal.

Now trains are electric. An electric rail runs next to the train track.

The electric rail powers the train.

Do you like to go on trains?